J
WAL

W9-AVO-175

Upchuck and the
Rotten Willy

Lex: 600
Pts: 4
Readl. 4.2

WITHDRAWN

JUN 0 0

Fulton Co. Public Library
320 W. 7th St.
Rochester, IN 46975

UPCHUCK
and the
ROTTEN
WILLY

Books by Bill Wallace

Red Dog
Trapped in Death Cave

Available From ARCHWAY Paperbacks

The Backward Bird Dog
Beauty
The Biggest Klutz in Fifth Grade
Blackwater Swamp
Buffalo Gal
The Christmas Spurs
Danger in Quicksand Swamp
Danger on Panther Peak
    (Original title: Shadow on the Snow)
A Dog Called Kitty
Ferret in the Bedroom, Lizards in the Fridge
The Final Freedom
Journey into Terror
Never Say Quit
Snot Stew
Totally Disgusting!
True Friends
Upchuck and the Rotten Willy
Watchdog and the Coyotes

Available from MINSTREL Books

BILL WALLACE

UPCHUCK
and the
ROTTEN
WILLY

ILLUSTRATED BY DAVID SLONIM

A MINSTREL® HARDCOVER
PUBLISHED BY POCKET BOOKS
New York London Toronto Sydney Tokyo Singapore

J
WAL
Wallace, Bill,
    Upchuck and the
    Rotten Willy

This book is a work of fiction. Names, characters, places and incidents are products of the author's imagination or are used fictitiously. Any resemblance to actual events or locales or persons living or dead is entirely coincidental.

A MINSTREL HARDCOVER

A Minstrel Book published by
POCKET BOOKS, a division of Simon & Schuster Inc.
1230 Avenue of the Americas, New York, NY 10020

Copyright © 1998 by Bill Wallace
Illustrations copyright © 1998 by David Slonim

All rights reserved, including the right to reproduce
this book or portions thereof in any form whatsoever.
For information address Pocket Books, 1230 Avenue
of the Americas, New York, NY 10020

ISBN: 0-671-01769-1

First Minstrel Books hardcover printing February 1998

10 9 8 7 6 5 4 3 2

A MINSTREL BOOK and colophon are registered trademarks of
Simon & Schuster Inc.

Printed in the U.S.A.   **3 3187 00151 9251**

UPCHUCK
and the
ROTTEN WILLY

14 Spurdist 16.00/8.96

CHAPTER 1

When the door closed behind me, I yawned and stretched. There were days I enjoyed sleeping late. This morning was crisp and cool, but not really cold. I was glad to be up. There was no wind. Not even the slightest breeze tickled the red and yellow leaves or rustled through dry, brown blades of grass. It wasn't often that the wind was still. I paused a moment, listening to the quiet, yet marveling at how many sounds there were.

Next door, Mrs. Parks told her husband to be careful driving to work and to bring home some chicken from the market for supper. Cars zoomed and rushed by on the big road near Luigi's Restaurant. Crows cawed from Farmer McVee's pecan orchard. Luigi's was over five blocks away, and Farmer McVee lived nearly a half-mile from our housing development. Still, the crows who raided his pecan trees sounded as close as if they were flying right over the top of my house.

I strolled around to the front yard and paused at the curb. Mr. Parks backed out of his driveway. I glanced both ways, to make sure there was nothing else on the road, then trotted across before he came in my direction.

At the alley behind Tom's house, I paused. Holding my breath, I moved nothing but my eyes. Once certain that Rocky was no place to be seen, I raced across the big, open grassy area toward the new high school. That's where my friend and I were to meet this morning.

It surprised me to find Tom already sitting on the wood fence between the baseball diamond and the football field.

Tom cocked an eyebrow and glanced down at me.

"About time you got up," he teased. "Been waiting on you for two hours."

"Have not." I frowned.

Tom smiled. "Would you believe, five minutes?"

We laughed.

He nodded at the wide wood rail beside him. "Come on . . ."—he paused a moment—". . . up Chuck."

The corners of my eyes tightened as I glared at him. But as I watched, I couldn't tell from the sly grin on his face whether he'd said it that way on purpose or by accident. Before I had a chance to figure it out, he turned his attention to the football field.

I hopped up next to him on the fence and leaned forward, trying to catch his eye.

"You do that on purpose?" I asked.

Tom ignored me. Still, I wasn't sure whether I could see a little glimmer in his eye or not. Without glancing at me, he motioned toward the field.

"Man, look at the haircut on that pink dude. You ever see anything so ridiculous in your life?" He chuckled.

I frowned and tilted my head to the side. "I think it's called apricot. Not pink."

"Apricot, pink," Tom shrugged. "Who cares? It's hilarious."

"Yeah," I nodded. "Talk about a 'bad-hair day.' "

"You know why their noses are so long and pointed?" Tom asked, only giving me a quick glance.

"No. Why?"

"So they can find—I mean, smell each other in the dark."

"Don't need to be dark," I managed with a

straight face. "They smell so bad you can find 'em any time of the day or night."

Tom nodded. "They sure do! They don't even have to be doing anything. I mean, all they've got to do is stand around—especially when it's hot. They got an odor to them, that's for sure."

"They're loud and rude, too. I mean, you get a group of them together . . ."

Tom nudged me with his shoulder. "All it takes for them to make a group is more than one."

"Yeah," I agreed. "Anyway, one at a time, they're bad enough. But you get a group together and you never heard so much noise. It's enough to wake the dead. Seems like, as big and floppy as their ears are, they wouldn't need to be that loud. But . . ."

"They sure are lazy," Tom interrupted. "One of them lived two doors down from the house I used to have before we moved here. All he did was lie around and sleep most of the day. Waited for somebody else to take care of him. They're rude, pushy, and mean. Shoot, they'd just as soon fight with one of their own as one of us. See that bunch near the far goalpost? See the way they're struttin' around and trying to look big and tough? You just watch. Sooner or later, they'll start a fight and . . ."

I nudged him so hard that he almost lost his

balance. "Look at this one coming around the track toward us," I said. "You know why his nose is so flat?"

"Why?"

"From chasing parked cars."

Tom's eyebrows scrunched down, like he was deep in thought. ". . . chasing parked cars . . ." he repeated, twitching his mouth to the side. At last he blinked. "Oh, I got it!"

Then he laughed, too. Both of us laughed so hard I thought we were gonna fall off the fence. We laughed and laughed and laughed.

"That was a great one, Chuck." He bumped his shoulder against mine. "A real classic. That's as good as the ones Louie used to come up with.

Suddenly, both of us stopped. The silence that grabbed us was instant—almost eerie. We looked at one another, then turned away—each somber and quiet in our own private thoughts.

It was the first time in three weeks that we had mentioned Louie's name. And though I'm sure Tom had thought about him as often as I had, neither of us ever talked about the horrible accident. We sat in silence for a long time. Neither of us looked at the other. Neither of us could find the right thing to say.

Finally, after what seemed an eternity, Tom nodded toward the football field again. The pink dude with the weird hair was the first to spot us.

He lunged and charged toward us, roaring and snapping, to bounce against the fence right below where we sat. The white dude who was with him followed right on his heels.

"Ah, pipe down," Tom hissed. "You two ain't so tough."

"Come down here," the white one barked. "We'll tear you apart."

"Look." Tom laughed. "Their haircuts make them look like they're wearing skirts."

"Yeah." I flipped my tail. "It looks like a little tutu. Ain't they cute? Hey, tutu-butt, why don't you do a little dance for us?"

The poodles barked a few more times before their master reached them. She got their leashes and dragged them back to the track. The commotion caused quite a stir. The group that was loose and acting tough with each other, down by the far goalpost, spotted us. Barking and roaring, they raced across the football field.

"Come on," Tom called as he leaped down from the fence. "That many of the nasty things coming after us, we better get going. Even as dumb as they are, one might accidentally find a way through the fence and get around behind us. Then we'd be trapped."

I jumped to the soft grass. Tails high, we chased across the baseball outfield, down the third-base line, and past home plate. We didn't even slow down to see if Rocky was out of his pen when we raced across the vacant lot between Tom's house and the high school athletic field. We squeezed through Tom's back gate and I followed him straight up the big pecan tree in his backyard.

Once safe and relaxed, we stretched out on a limb to clean up and wash our faces with our paws.

Tom and Louie had been my best friends for as long as I could remember. Well, not as long as I could remember, but ever since I was old enough that the people I lived with started letting me go outside. A little over two months ago, Louie found out that people brought their dogs to the track around the new high school football field. The people walked around the track for exercise. Most kept their dogs on a leash, but others just let them run loose. Every Saturday for a whole month, Louie, Tom, and I met on the fence between the ball diamond and the football field to watch them and make fun of the dogs.

I didn't really have all that much against dogs. Still, it was a regular riot to sit around and tell jokes about them, or make fun of the way they looked and acted.

It was great to have a best friend. I was one

lucky cat. I had had two best friends. Louie and Tom were the *best* best friends anyone could ever ask for. Nothing could ever come between us. Nothing could ever separate us. It just wouldn't be fair.

But . . . nobody ever told me life was fair.

CHAPTER 2

We spent a while soaking up the morning sunshine. It was beautiful day. After a time, the wind picked up and shook our limb.

I looked over at my best friend. His eyes were closed, but every now and then his ear twitched when the wind tickled the little hairs down inside. I moved closer. He peeked out of one eye when he felt the limb bend under my weight. I sat down and curled my tail under my bottom.

"We need to talk."

"So talk," he purred and closed his eye. "Got a new dog-joke you just thought up?"

Even though his eyes were closed and he couldn't see me, I shook my head.

"No. I mean *really* talk."

He cocked his eye again. "About what?"

I took a deep breath and sighed.

"Louie."

Tom curled tighter into his ball. "I don't want to talk about Louie. I don't even want to think about him."

I moved closer.

"Please."

"No."

"Why?"

"Because!"

His tail flipped around to cover his eye. I reached out a paw and pulled it aside. The eye popped open. The yellow slit that ran up and down in the middle grew so tight it glowed like a streak of fire.

"Why?" I repeated.

For only an instant, the fur puffed up on his tail. He took a deep breath and sighed. When he did, the hair smoothed down.

"It hurts too much to talk about him. I try my best not to even think about him. He was a good cat. He was fun to be with. He ran out in the street and got hit by a car. Now he's dead. There's nothing else to say."

With that, he closed his eye and wrapped his tail back over his head. I sat for a long time, watching him. Thinking. Maybe there *was* nothing else to say. Maybe it was best to forget our friend—there was nothing we could do for him.

There was no way we could change what had happened. So, if Tom didn't want to talk about him, that was fine.

My tail flipped to one side so hard that it almost knocked me off balance. My claws sprang out to hold on to the limb.

If Tom didn't want to talk about him, that was fine. *I did!* I wanted to talk about Louie. I *needed* to talk about Louie. If Tom didn't want to listen—well, that was up to him.

"He *was* fun to be with." I echoed what Tom had said. "He was a good cat and he was fun. I remember that Pomeranian from over on Sixth Street. When he sneaked out of his yard and came strutting past Luigi's Restaurant . . . man, he was acting like he owned the place. Figured he could just up and help himself to our spaghetti and meatballs. We started to run, but Louie just marched right up to him. Stared him square in the eye. Then he marched around and stared at the other end. With the little puff of hair on his head and the way his tail flipped up, Louie says: 'I'd scratch this guy on the nose, but Pomeranians are so ugly, can't tell whether he's coming or going. Don't know which end to scratch.' "

Tom didn't say anything.

"Then there was that time over in Rocky's back yard . . ."

"That was dumb," Tom said, without opening his eye.

"No, it wasn't. He didn't mean to fall out of the pecan tree and land in Rocky's food bowl. It was an accident."

Tom peeked up at me. "I know he didn't mean to fall. It was what he did *afterward.*"

"Yeah." I kind of laughed to myself. "It was cool, though. I mean, Rocky saw him go *kerplop*—right in the middle of his food dish—so he came flying after him."

"If Louie hadn't landed on his feet," Tom unwrapped his tail from around his face and sat up, "Rocky would have got him for sure."

"Louie *always* landed on his feet." I smiled. "Always."

Tom licked a paw and smoothed his whiskers. "Even landing on his feet, it was a close call. He just squeezed through the crack in the gate a half second before that dog got there. If he'd brushed so much as a whisker and slowed down, Rocky would have had him. It was *that* close."

My tail flopped back and forth as I laughed.

"It was so close, Rocky didn't have time to stop. Got his head through the crack—and that was it. Stopped like the rest of him had hit a brick wall. Stuck there, and all he could do was bark and yap and tell Louie what he was gonna do to him when he got loose."

"Prancing back and forth in front of him and teasing him was bad enough," Tom said. Now his tail was flipping back and forth, like mine was. "But when he climbed back over the fence and started swatting Rocky on the behind . . . Never saw anything so funny in my life!"

"And remember that time . . ."

The memories of our friend *did* make us feel better. We spent the rest of the morning talking and remembering all the good times we had had together.

Louie didn't have people like Tom and I did. He was an alley cat. The only people he even had anything to do with was Luigi. That's who he took his name from—Louie—Luigi.

Luigi was kind of round and plump. He had dark eyes and dark hair and a long mustache that drooped down under his nose. He wore a white apron that always had tomato sauce smudged on it. His tummy bounced up and down underneath the apron when he laughed. And he always laughed when Louie came to ask for food. The first time Louie took us there, Luigi laughed at us, too. He seemed to take great pride when we ate the plate of spaghetti and meatballs he set out for us. Especially when we gobbled all of it and licked the platter clean.

We talked about how smart and quick Louie was, and what a great sense of humor he had. Being an alley cat, he had a strong distaste for dogs. Neither Tom nor I had ever thought much about dogs. Not until we started running around with Louie. Some of the neat things he could think up to say about them were absolutely hilarious.

We talked and talked and talked. We talked or thought about everything, from the first time we had met Louie until that day we found him all smushed up near the curb by the shopping mall. We still missed him, but talking about all the good times seemed to make us feel better.

Tom stood up and arched his back. "Wonder what time it is. I'm getting kind of hungry."

How long we sat and talked, I didn't know. I was hungry, too. I stretched the kinks out of my back. "Been a long time since we've seen Luigi. Bet he misses Louie. Let's go say hi to him and see if he'll still feed us."

The branch where we visited was a low one. Tom leaped to the ground and patted the grass with his paw.

"Come on . . ." he paused, "up Chuck."

A puff of red exploded before my eyes. This time, I knew he did it on purpose. He was down—not up. My tail puffed as big around as a balloon. Claws sprang out, and my eyes squinted to tiny slits. In a rage, I flew from the tree and slammed into him.

The force of my attack knocked him over. Hissing and spitting and scratching, we tumbled clear across Tom's backyard.

CHAPTER 3

The fight didn't last very long.

We rolled around under the tree for a while. Tom got to his feet and took off. I was hot on his heels. He faked one way, then turned the other. As soon as he turned, I leaped and rolled him again. I bit him once, but that was about it. Aside from the hissing and scuffling, it really wasn't much of a fight.

It's kind of hard to rip somebody to shreds when they're laughing their fur off. I was mad and ready to tear Tom apart. Only when he didn't fight back and just kept laughing . . . well . . .

"I really *do* wish you'd quit with that 'Up-chuck' stuff," I panted.

Tom ruffled his fur and used his hind foot to

17

scratch the place where I'd bitten him behind the ear.

"Oh, lighten up," he laughed. "Can't believe you get so bent out of shape over your stupid name."

"It's *not* my name! It's a nickname, and I hate it!" As I thought about it—remembered—my tail flipped one way, then the other. I didn't flip it. It was kind of like my tail had a mind of its own and it flipped itself. "When I came to live with my Katie, she was dating this guy named Chuck." My tail jerked so hard I had to move my hind foot to keep my balance. Tom stopped scratching behind his ear and leaned toward me.

"Wait a minute," he interrupted. "I know you've told me this before, but go through that dating stuff again. I'm still not too clear on what dating is."

"Okay. She thought this guy was really cute and all that stuff. I guess he liked her, too. Anyway, when a boy-people and a girl-people like each other, they go out on dates."

"Like?" He arched an eyebrow.

"Like they go out and eat, or they go to a show, or they just sit on the porch and hold paws."

"What's a show?"

"I don't know."

"Well, you got an idea."

"Okay." I sighed. "I think it's kind of like the Noisy Box in the living room . . . you know?"

Tom nodded. "Yeah, my people have one, too. They sit in front of the thing a bunch. I don't know why, but they just sit there with their mouths open and look dumb. Right?"

"Right. Anyway, I think a movie is kind of like that, only bigger. And instead of one or two people watching it, there must be a whole bunch, because when they got home I could always smell lots of people and popcorn all over them. Katie would talk about how good the show was, and about buildings blowing up or people shooting each other or kissing and romance—all that junk."

Tom stretched out and rested his chin on his paws. "Okay. I think I'm with you. But why do they do that?"

My tail flipped so hard it jerked my rear end the other way.

"I don't know. They just *do*. Anyway, she liked this guy named Chuck, and they were dating when I came to live with her—so, she named me Chuck. Then she and Chuck decided they didn't like each other anymore, so they broke up and she started dating Jimmy."

"Only Jimmy didn't like Chuck, right?"

"Right," I nodded. "Every time Katie talked about Chuck, Jimmy would give off this mad smell and his eyes would kind of scrunch up. If I was around, or if Katie wanted me to come so she could pet me or scratch behind my ears, she'd call, 'Here, Chuck. Here, Chuck,' and Jimmy would get mad. Every time he so much as looked at me, he'd give off that mad smell."

"And you threw up on him, so he changed your name to Upchuck?"

"No!" My lips curled back so my teeth showed, and I hissed at him. "I didn't throw up on *him*. It was his convertible. And it wasn't my fault. When they came home from a date, he always parked it next to the carport. In the evenings, I like to sit on the roof. It was easier to jump to the car, then to the ground. So I'd wait for them to come home. It was kind of fun to sit on the roof until my Katie and Jimmy were hugging on one another or playing kissy-face—you know, when they weren't paying attention. Then I'd land on the soft, cloth roof of his convertible and they'd both jerk like they'd been shot.

"But this one day, the Mama changed my food. The new food was really good. So instead of eating part of it at supper time and then coming back for a midnight snack—I ended up gobbling the whole can down in one sitting. Trouble was, the new food really upset my stomach. I was just about to jump down and go eat some grass—you know, to settle my stomach? But right then,

Jimmy drove up. Well, I was feeling really bad, so as soon as he stopped, I jumped to his roof. Only he didn't have the roof up. I mean, I was in midair before I noticed there was no roof to land on. Well, that scared me—and, along with already being sick to my stomach . . . I . . . well, I landed in the backseat. And . . . well . . . the minute I landed, I threw up."

"All over his backseat." Tom licked a paw and smoothed his whiskers.

"All over his backseat," I repeated with a sigh. "That's when he started calling me Upchuck. I didn't mind him doing it, but when my Katie would tease me and call me that . . . it really hurt." I noticed that my tail had stopped flipping. I curled it to the side and sat down. "I don't know why people make such a big fuss about throwing up. I mean, it's as natural as eating or going to the bathroom or chasing mice. Why do they get so bent out of shape over something that natural?"

Tom shook his head.

"People-animals are just weird. I went to my drinking bowl the other day, but my Pat forgot to fill it up. So I went to the bathroom to get a drink from the big drinking bowl. She came running in, screaming and yelling at me. They're just weird."

We laid around, talking about people-animals and how strange they acted. Tom said that when

people-animals tease, it means they really like you, and they aren't being mean. He told me I shouldn't get so upset about my nickname. We talked about my Katie getting ready to leave for a place called college, and we wondered what that could be. We talked about growing up and chasing mice and all sorts of things. When the conversation finally got around to food, we remembered that we were headed to Luigi's when the fight started. Suddenly, both of us were starving again.

Tom leaped to his feet and scampered up the tree.

"Come on," he meowed. "Let's take the short-cut over Rocky's yard."

"I don't like going over Rocky's," I said.

"Why not? There's hardly any wind. We can make it."

"Let's go the regular way," I insisted. "It's safer."

There was a mischievous twinkle in Tom's eyes. "Don't be such a sissy. We can make it." He licked his lips, smiled, and patted the branch beside him.

"Come on . . . up . . . Chuck."

CHAPTER 4

There was an enormous, old pecan tree in Tom's backyard. The branches were so long and flowing that they covered most of his yard and spread out over half of Rocky's yard. Rocky was the Doberman who lived next door. Mr. and Mrs. Edwards lived on the far side of Rocky's yard. They were retired. That meant they were kind of old and didn't go to the office. They just stayed home. But the truth of the matter—lately they didn't even stay home much. That was because they had this huge car thing that looked like a house inside. They were always gone, running around to visit family or just vacationing in a place called Florida or another place called Arizona. (I wondered if Florida and Arizona were like our neighborhood.) There was a big sign in their front yard. But since cats can't read, I didn't pay much attention to it. The sign stayed for a couple of weeks, but, like the Edwards, now it was gone, too.

Anyhow, they also had an enormous, old pecan tree in their backyard. Its branches were so long and flowing that they covered most of the Edwards' backyard and half of Rocky's.

Right over the center of Rocky's yard, a big limb from the Edwards' pecan tree met a big limb from Tom's pecan tree. They were so close that they almost touched. Fact was, if the wind blew really hard from the north, sometimes they did clunk together. If we were real careful, and if the wind wasn't blowing, we could leap from one branch to the other—kind of like a skywalk to get from one yard to the other without getting near Rocky.

I chased Tom up his pecan tree. We circled round and round the trunk before he broke clear to the top. I almost got him once, when he reached the small branches. Near the top of the tree the limbs were so little and limber that they bent under his weight. He climbed just a bit too high. When the limb bent, I swatted, but I only got a little tuft of hair from his tail.

Tom leaped to a bigger limb and came back down the other side of the tree. I was right behind him when he raced out onto the huge branch, made the jump, and raced across the Edwards' tree. I didn't even think about how dangerous it was. Not until Rocky jumped against the fence, right under me.

His roaring bark and the way the board cracked when he threw himself against it made me freeze in my tracks. Claws out, I held onto the branch with my death-grip and looked down.

Rocky was right under me. Again and again he leaped. White fangs snapped and slashed just inches from my paws. My tail exploded in a puff of fur that was as big around as I was. I couldn't move. I couldn't even breathe.

"I got you now, you stinking cat," he snarled. "If I could . . ." He jumped and snapped. ". . . just jump a little . . ." He jumped again and snapped. ". . . higher, I'd chew you up and . . ."

Every time he jumped, he made another threat.

". . . and eat you for . . . supper . . . I'd bite your . . . tail off and . . . use it to stir my . . . dog food . . . and I'd . . ."

He must have jumped and threatened ten times before Tom finally came back for me.

"Quit pestering that stupid dog," he scolded, walking out to meet me on the limb. "You keep standing here, he's gonna have a heart attack. Now, come on."

I guess I was more scared than I thought. Tom's words seemed to snap me out of my trance. With one eye on the limb and one eye on Rocky's snapping jaws and flashing fangs, I followed my friend.

At the fork in the tree where the branch joined the trunk, I stopped. Guess I held my breath longer than I thought, 'cause all I could do was stand there, panting and gasping for air. Rocky kept leaping and snarling his threats behind me. Each time he jumped, I could see the tip of his pointy nose and his pointy ears. Since he was on the far side of the wood fence, that was about all. Tom backed down the trunk of the pecan tree. A few feet from the ground he turned, jumped, and headed for the far side of the yard.

The Edwards had a wood fence like Tom, Rocky, and the rest of the houses on the block. But since they were on the corner, they had a big, double gate on the side next to the road. It was never closed, though. That was because it was where they parked their huge car thing that looked like a house on the inside.

Still panting, I began licking my paw and washing my face. I noticed the gate was closed. I never saw it closed before, but I didn't give it much thought. My heart was still pounding inside my chest. Maybe a good face-washing would calm me—get the fur on my tail to flatten and get my heart to stop thumping so hard.

Then . . . all of a sudden . . . my heart stopped!

The breath caught in my throat!

I had licked my paw and was bringing it toward my whiskers. It stopped, too!

Everything stopped! Everything froze in that instant of time when I saw it.

It was *EEEnormous!*

A monster! A big, hairy beast! And it was sneaking across the Edwards' yard, toward my friend.

Big as a car and black as death itself, the giant moved closer! I opened my mouth to meow—to scream and warn Tom.

No sound came out!

My heart started to beat again. It pounded in my chest.

Watching me, Tom didn't notice the gate was closed. He didn't see the huge, black, ugly beast.

It was like watching a dream. No—a nightmare. There was nothing I could do. The giant animal was close. One lunge and he'd have my friend. One quick move and the nightmare would end. I couldn't watch. It would be too horrible. Too terrible to see.

Only, my eyes wouldn't close. No matter how I tried to force them, they stayed wide.

Tom stopped. He tilted his head and looked up at me. He swished his tail from side to side.

The beast stopped. He leaned forward.

In my mind's eye, I could see those white fangs. I could picture the gaping cavern of his mouth—those powerful jaws snapping shut on my friend. The huge monster leaned closer. Closer.

Then . . .

CHAPTER 5

Then . . .

He sniffed.

That's it—he just sniffed.

The beast's nostrils were so wide, his sniff made the hair stand out on Tom's side. If Tom hadn't flipped his tail in the other direction, it would have been sucked into the powerful wind tunnel of the monster's nose.

Tom, feeling something, twitched and gave a little shudder. The monster sniffed again. More hair stood out on Tom's side.

Irritated, he glanced over his shoulder.

I've never heard a cat scream.

I've heard cats meow, snarl, hiss, spit, howl, and yowl. But I've never heard a cat scream.

*   *   *

Tom screamed. The instant he saw the colossal monster, his eyes popped wide and he screamed. He screamed when he saw him. He screamed when he spun and raced toward the tree. He screamed as he passed the branch where I sat, frozen and watching the entire scene. He never stopped screaming—not even after he raced to the top of the tree and hung, dangling by one paw, from a tiny branch at the very tip.

The little limb was barely big enough to hold the single pecan that grew at its end. Still, Tom managed to hang on to the thing as it bent, almost double, beneath his weight.

The monster's mouth flopped open. (Guess he'd never heard a cat scream, either.) His ears arched up. His brow scrunched down. His head tilted to the side and he sat on his stubby tail.

I raced to the top of the tree to help my friend. It took a lot of talking and pleading to get Tom to let go of his limb and climb to join me on a bigger, more sturdy one. It took a lot more time before his fur began to smooth. For a while, Tom was more than twice as big as Tom. I never saw anybody puff up like that. Even after he began to calm down, there was still a ridge of hair from his shoulders to his tail that stood on end and wouldn't relax.

"What was it?" he gasped, finally.

"Don't know. I never saw anything like it."

Fulton Co. Public Library
320 W. 7th St.
Rochester, IN 46975

We looked down. The beast sat watching us. He still had his head cocked and that confused look on his face.

"I think it's a dog," Tom wheezed.

I shook my head so hard my ears flopped.

"Can't be a dog. It's too big. It must be a bear."

"What's a bear?"

"It's a dog, only bigger. They're wild and they live in the woods. They eat honey and fish."

"Not cats?"

When I swallowed, my throat made a gulping sound. "I don't know."

We eased over to a bigger branch. Then, claws out and our hold tight, we moved down the trunk of the pecan to an even larger limb.

Inch at a time, Tom moved out on the branch that hung over the Edwards'—I mean, the monster's yard. He didn't walk on the branch, he lay on his tummy and wrapped his front and back arms around the limb as he crawled forward.

"What in the world are you?" Tom called down to the monster.

The beast's mouth tightened to a tiny grin.

"I'm Willy."

"What's a willy?"

The beast cocked his head in the other direction.

"Huh?"

"What's a willy?" Tom repeated.

"Willy's not a what, it's a who. That's my name. Willy."

Clinging to the same branch, I crawled on my tummy. With my claws out and my arms wrapped around the limb, I scooted up behind my friend. I peeked over the side.

"You're a bear, right?"

"No!" His brow scrunched down and his ears almost folded over his face. "I'm a Rott."

My tail flipped. It tried to get hold of the branch, too.

"A rotten what?"

"A Rotten Willy," Tom whispered from in front of me.

"A Rotten Willy?"

"I think that's what he said." He looked down. "Did you say a Rotten Willy?"

The beast flopped his head so hard, his jowls made a popping sound.

"No! A Rott. It's short for Rottweiler."

"What's that?" Tom and I both asked at once.

"It's my breed. I'm a Rottweiler."

"But what's a Rottweiler?"

"I'm a dog. A Rottweiler dog. And my name is Willy."

Tom stood on the branch. He turned to me, curled his tail under, and sat down. "That's no dog! I've seen a lot of dogs in my life, and that thing isn't a dog. No way does a dog get that big."

"I *am* a dog," the plaintive voice came from below us.

Tom shook his head and looked me square in the eye. "I went with Louie one time over to Farmer McVee's place. They got this horse called a Shetland pony." He glanced down at the beast below our branch. "This thing is as big as a horse. No way does a dog get as big as a horse."

A little whimpering sound came from below.

"But I *am* a dog. Honest."

Tom leaned close to my ear.

"I don't know what he is, but he's not a dog. You don't think Rotten Willies can . . ."

Tom stopped right in the middle of his sentence. His eyes got real wide. We both peeked over the branch. The gigantic monster—the Rotten Willy—sat there, looking up at us. Tom's eyes got even wider.

"Can what?" I asked, hoping he'd finish what he was about to say.

Suddenly, Tom took off. He leaped clear over me.

I jumped to my feet and turned. "Rotten Willies can *what?*" I called after him.

Tom raced across the limb. Rocky charged from his bed on the back porch. He roared and barked his threats when Tom leaped from the Edwards' pecan tree to his own tree.

I felt trapped. The Rotten Willy stood beneath my limb, looking lost and confused. Rocky leaped against the wood fence on Tom's side of the yard, roaring and barking his threats. I was stuck here, with no idea what had made Tom take off like he did.

"What if Rotten Willies can *what?*" I called one last time.

Tom stood in the fork of his pecan tree. He was all fuzzed up again. His eyes were big, and he was panting for breath.

"I just had a terrible thought," he called to me. "What if Rotten Willies can climb trees?"

CHAPTER 6

It was a terrible thought.

I looked down at the bulky monster beneath the tree. He was black as night, with brown around his belly and mouth—a mouth full of teeth, with powerful jaws. What if he *could* climb? If he really was a dog, like he said, there was no problem. It's common knowledge that dogs are too stupid to climb trees. But what if he'd lied to us? What if he really wasn't a dog? What if he was some strange thing called a Rotten Willy? And . . . what if Rotten Willies *could climb* trees?

A chill raced through me. It started around my ears and crawled down my back, clean to the tip of my tail.

Carefully, one step at a time, I worked my way

along the branch. With almost every step, I would pause and glance down at him. The Rotten Willy just sat there with his head cocked and watched me.

One false move and . . .

WHAM!

My eyes flashed when I looked around. Rocky leaped against the fence, right beneath my paws. I heard the loud *wham* again.

"Got you now, you stupid . . . cat . . ." He leaped and snarled his threats. "I'm gonna chew . . . you in half. And . . . I'm gonna mush you up . . . into little pieces . . . and . . ."

The fur puffed up and stood out straight where every chill bump had been. I couldn't move.

Behind me was the Rotten Willy. For all I knew, he was already climbing the tree—already closing in for the kill. Beneath me was Rocky. The limb from the Edwards'—I mean, the Rotten Willy's tree—swooped lower and lower before it crossed the big branch to Tom's tree. One slip and I was a goner.

"Come on, Chuck," Tom called from his tree.

"I can't. I'm scared."

"You can make it," he encouraged. "Rocky can't get you. He's just making noise."

"But what if I slip? What if I miss the jump?"

Tom arched his back.

"Quit being such a wimp. Come on."

"But—"

"Don't be a sissy," he hissed, cutting me off. "Go for it. Just keep walking."

I felt my legs tremble beneath me. Inside my head I told them to move, but they wouldn't.

"I . . . I don't think . . . I can," I stammered.

"Go! Come on." He paused for only a moment. "Come on, Upchuck."

This time, he didn't even hesitate between the "up" and the "Chuck."

"Don't do that, Tom," I meowed back at him. "Don't tease me. Not now. I'm really scared."

"Upchuck's a sissy. Upchuck's a sissy," he began to sing.

"Please," I pleaded.

"Upchuck. Upchuck. Upchuck."

My eyes tightened. My claws dug deeper into the tree bark. My lip curled.

Rocky leaped and snarled. I never heard him. Someplace behind me, the black hulk of the Rotten Willy was probably sneaking closer and closer. I never gave him another thought. My eyes were on Tom. *My friend!*

When I finally made it to the fork in Tom's tree where *my friend* stood, I expected him to leap to his yard and go running off, with me chasing him.

He didn't.

Instead, he rushed over to me. Purring, he rubbed his cheek against mine. "Knew you could do it, Chuck," he lulled. "You just got to have a little confidence in yourself. I knew you could make it. When you freeze like that, it really scares me. Don't scare me like that anymore, okay?" He purred. "If we ever go back over Rocky's yard, just keep walking. Don't even think about him. Don't look down. Just go."

We rubbed on each other for a while. Tom kept reminding me that I was a cat. Cats are sure-footed and brave and smart—not at all like dogs. And he told me that I was one of the bravest and smartest and most surefooted cats he had ever met. He explained that the only reason he called me Upchuck was because he knew it would make me mad enough to come after him instead of thinking about Rocky. He told me that I was the *best* best friend he could ever have.

Tom was the *best* best friend I could ever have, too. He was always there for me when I needed him. Nobody wants to be a fraidycat. Tom kept me from being one. He helped me and made me feel brave and strong.

We left his yard and headed to Luigi's Restaurant. Tom and I put on quite a show. The back screen door was shut to keep the flies out. Both of us bumped against the wood part of the screen door to knock and let Luigi know we were there. When he didn't come, Tom jumped up on the screen. Clinging with his claws in the wire mesh, he jerked and rattled the door until Luigi finally came.

When the plump man with the white apron opened the screen, Tom jumped down. As soon as he stepped outside, we both began to rub against his legs. We purred and circled and circled and purred.

"Hey, how's my boys?" He greeted us with his rumbling laugh. "Long time, no see."

He frowned and looked around.

"Where's my little Louie? He not come with you today?"

"He got smushed by a car," Tom answered.

"Maybe he find him a new home. But Luigi bet his new home not fix good spaghetti and meatballs, like Luigi."

As usual, people-animals just don't listen. Luigi kept looking around. Finally he gave a big shrug. With a smile that made the corners of his dark, black whiskers turn up at the ends, he bent down and laughed. He patted Tom on the back and scratched me behind the ears. It felt good. His warm, rumbly laugh felt good, too.

"You no visit Luigi. What? Been busy chasing mouses, huh? Bet you starved for Luigi's good cookin'." He shoved us away from the screen

with his foot. "You wait here. Luigi fix plenty good meat sauce—just for you."

I don't think Tom or I, either one, were that hungry. But *nobody* could pass up Luigi's spaghetti and meatballs. He plopped a big plate in front of us and wiped sauce on his white apron. (It matched the rest of the stains.) His deep, rumbling laugh seemed to shake the trash can by the back door when he watched us dig in. He petted us a moment, asked again about Louie, then went back to his cooking. Tom and I ate until we were about to explode.

I'm one lucky cat! I thought as I gobbled a delicious meatball. I had my Katie. I had Luigi. Best of all—I had Tom. Best friends just don't come any better than that. And I knew we'd stay best friends . . . forever.

Chapter 7

I wonder how long forever is.

It was a people word. The first time I heard it was when my Katie and Chuck held paws and played kissy-face on the front porch. They told each other they would be together—forever.

Chuck didn't stay around very long.

My Katie and Jimmy said the same stuff about being in love—forever. Jimmy had been around for a long time. A lot longer than I liked.

Come to think of it, I didn't really know how long forever was. I thought it was a long, long time. Maybe it wasn't. Maybe people didn't know how long forever was, either—and people-animals know a lot. They can talk with mouth noises and they can even read signs and stuff.

That's a lot. But maybe nobody knows how long forever is.

Maybe it wasn't as long as I thought.

On the way back home, we didn't bound and leap across the vacant field behind my house—we waddled. At the street, Tom stopped and looked both ways. Then we waddled across. We waddled clear to his front porch where we sat and washed our faces with our paws.

To be honest, I didn't wash my face too well. I had sucked a really long piece of spaghetti into my mouth. The tail end of it flipped me on the eyebrow. I cleaned that off, as well as the gooey red stuff near my ears. But I left some of the meat sauce on my whiskers. That way, when I licked my lips, I could taste it all day. We curled up and slept in the sun for the rest of the afternoon.

It was the very next day when "forever" started getting shorter and shorter.

My Katie left.

My Katie had left before. I had come to live with her when I was just a kitten. Almost every day, she had left for a place called school. She told me she was a Senior and that "seniors are really cool." I didn't know what a senior was, but being one made my Katie happy—so I was happy, too.

Going to school had been okay. When my Katie had come home, she played with me. She dragged an old sock round and round on her bed while I chased it. She hugged me and petted me and rubbed behind my ears. At night I slept on the pillow, next to her. Then, after a few months, my Katie had told me she was a "Glad You Ate." Now, I had no idea what a glad you ate was. My Katie had told me that she was happy to be one— only us cats don't just listen with our ears. We watch and feel and smell. My Katie made the mouth noises that *said* she was happy, only the feel she gave off said she was happy and sad and worried, all rolled together. She smelled confused and uncertain—like maybe being a senior had been more fun than being a glad you ate—only she didn't know for sure.

The thing I knew for sure, was that she stayed home with me for three whole weeks. She didn't have to go to her school place and she slept late and petted me and played with me and gave me table scraps.

But after three weeks, my Katie had gone to work. I didn't know what work was either, but the Mama and Daddy went to work. Now my Katie went to work, too.

Work was kind of a mixed-up thing. Like glad you ate and school, work brought her home with strange feelings. Some days when she got home,

I could feel the happy on my Katie. Other days, I could only feel irritation and mad. But every day I could feel tired on her. Even more tired than school.

Still, work wasn't all that bad. After an hour or so of rest, my Katie would play with me or pet me while she watched the Noisy Box in the living room. Other times, Jimmy would come over and they would go on a "date," or hold paws and play kissy-face. At night, she would take me to bed with her, and I'd curl up on our pillow.

But for the last two weeks, my Katie and the Mama and Daddy had been talking about "college." When they had talked of college, it smelled and felt a lot like school—only different somehow. Even with my keen cat-sense of smell and feel, I couldn't quite put my claw on what college really meant.

For two weeks, they had talked about it. The next week, my Katie had put clothes and stuff in boxes. (That had made me a little nervous, but my Katie had put stuff in boxes before.) The last two days, she had spent a whole lot of time hugging me and petting me and saying sweet things to me.

Then, she left.

Like senior school and glad you ate and work, I had expected her to come home every evening.

She didn't.

*   *   *

The Mama and Daddy were nice to me. She fed me and petted me. He scratched behind my ears if I jumped in his lap while he was reading his paper. But they weren't my Katie. They didn't love me or play with me. Worst of all, I had to sleep all by myself. I didn't like that. I didn't understand.

"How would *I* know what college is?" Tom answered, swishing his tail. "I've never been there. I've never even heard the word before."

He walked beneath the branch where I lay and rubbed his side on the trunk of the pecan tree. Then he lay down on the grass and used the ground to scratch his ear.

"College must be far away," I mused, lying on the branch that forked out from the pecan's trunk. The big limb wasn't far off the ground. When Tom got up to rub his side against the bark, I swatted at his tail. It was just out of reach.

"If it was close, my Katie would come home. College must be mean, too. Maybe it's like a cage. Maybe the college thing has her locked up and won't let her out to play or come home. I wish I knew."

Feeling sad and lonely, I gazed up through the leaves at the blue sky. "I wish I knew if my Katie was all right. I wish I knew what college was."

"I know."

The voice startled me. It came from beneath my branch—where Tom was. Only the sound was deep and rumbly. It was not Tom. Soft and gentle, the strange voice was totally unexpected, and it made me jump.

"Who said that" I demanded, looking down. I couldn't see anything.

"I did."

I leaned over to peek on the other side of the branch where I sat.

Tom screamed. He screamed when he jumped from the ground to the pecan tree. He screamed when he clawed his way past my branch and raced toward the top of the tree. He screamed clear until he reached a tiny limb at the very tip that bent under his weight. There he dangled by one claw—holding on for his life.

I'd never heard a cat scream before. I'd heard them meow and howl and . . .

Suddenly, my eyes popped wide.

I *had* heard a cat scream. I remembered, now . . .

Claws out, I leaned farther to the side. An enormous black face with brown around the eyes and mouth—it was—it was right there beside me! Huge jaws were almost even with my hind end. A brown eye was so close, it could have touched my tail.

It was the Rotten Willy!

51

Chapter 8

Mama, help! Mama, help!" Tom yowled from above me.

"You really should get him down," the Rotten Willy said from below me. "The limb isn't big enough to hold him. He's gonna fall and get hurt."

Tom dangled by one claw from a tiny limb at the very tip of the pecan tree. The Rotten Willy stood up on his hind legs, with his front paws on the limb where I had been sitting only a second before. I clung to the pecan tree about halfway between them.

"Mama, help!" Tom yowled again.

"You better hurry. That limb's about to go."

I looked down at the Rotten Willy. I looked up at Tom, then down again. Suddenly, a thought hit me.

"He's scared," I said. "He won't listen to me. Why don't *you* go get him?"

The Rotten Willy tilted his head to the side. "Huh?"

"You climb up and get him."

"I can't."

"Why not?"

The Rotten Willy shook his head and his ears flopped. "I'm a dog. Dogs can't climb trees." He held up a paw. "See? Our claws aren't long enough. No grip on the bark." Suddenly, his eyes got big and round. "Whoops—too late!"

There was a cracking sound. I looked up just in time to see Tom fall. He didn't land on his feet, like Louie always did. He hit the branch below him on his back. All four feet clawed the air, grabbing for anything. The limb bent under his weight, then it sprang upward. It flipped Tom head over tail. Rear end spinning, he flew through the air to a lower limb, missed it, and finally caught himself on the next branch.

Eyes wide and gasping for air, he clung there until he had his balance. Once his feet were under him and his claws deep into the wood, he looked around.

"What? Where?"

"You okay?" I meowed.

"What happened? Where am I?"

"In your pecan tree," I answered. "Fifth branch from the top. Are you okay?"

"I . . . I think so. I . . . er . . . yes, I'm okay. Are you okay, Chuck? The Rotten Willy didn't get you, did he?"

"I'm right here," I soothed. "He didn't get me." I frowned at the enormous monster, who was still watching us. "What are you doing in Tom's yard? Why are you here?"

"I'm here because of college."

My ears twitched. Cautiously, I relaxed my grip on the tree trunk, backed down a ways and turned to sit on a branch. It was a good ways above the ground, and I felt safe. No matter how big the Rotten Willy was, he couldn't possibly jump this high.

"What do you mean, you're here because of college?"

His ears shrugged. "I was walking down the alley and I heard you talking about college. That's why I came over. I didn't mean to scare you."

My tail flipped to the other side of the branch.

"But the Edwards' yard, I mean, your yard has a fence around it. How did you get out?"

I couldn't help but notice the brown around his huge mouth when he smiled.

"I guess that's because of college, too."

I moved down, one more branch, but still out

of his reach. Above me, I could hear Tom's claws scratching the bark as he came to join me. I leaned over and looked down at the Rotten Willy.

"What do you mean—because of college?"

"David. That's my boy. He went to college, last year. I sure do miss him. He used to play with me, and pet me, and take me for walks and stuff. With him gone to college, I get bored. When there's nothing for me to do, I dig. I dug under my fence to go explore. As I was walking up the alley, I heard you and Tom talking about college. The back gate was open, so I thought I'd stop by."

Still trembling, Tom moved beside me on the branch. I ignored him and watched the Rotten Willy.

"Do you know what college is?"

"Yep." He let go of the tree with his front paws and sat on his stubby tail. "Well, I've been there, and I've seen what it looks like, but I still don't know for sure what it is."

"Where is it? Is it far away?"

"Yep. Pretty far." His upper lip flopped when he nodded his head. "The first day, all of us went to move my David's clothes and toys. We rode half a day in the car just to get there."

"Is it mean? Is college like a cage and it won't let people out?"

"I don't think it's mean. My David stayed there for three whole weeks before he came home for the first time. So, I guess it's not like a cage. I guess he could come home whenever he wanted. I don't think he liked it—not at first. When he came home, I could feel scared and unhappy on him. He even told the Mama that he didn't like college and he missed the Mama and Daddy. But the next time he came home, it was better. After that I could even feel happy—happy to be home, then happy when he was going back."

"What's it like?" I asked, backing down the trunk to a lower limb.

"It's sort of like 'go to school,' only really big. There are lots of buildings and lots of people. And, instead of coming home at night, they stay there." He lowered his head and made a little *whoompf* sound. "That's the part I don't like. It was a lot more fun when my David would come home from school and play with me."

I moved a little closer and sat on a limb.

"Chuck," I heard Tom whisper. "Chuck."

I ignored him. "Did you sleep with your David?"

"Chuck." Tom's whisper was louder.

"No. I sleep outside."

"That's what I really miss." I felt my whiskers droop. "I always sleep with my Katie at night. I sure do miss . . ."

"Chuck!" Tom's whisper was so loud it sounded like a buzz saw.

". . . miss having someone to sleep with at night," I went right on, still doing my best to ignore him. "Us cats see really good in the dark— lots better than people do. I always slept real light, so I could guard my Katie. So I could protect her. I was never scared of the dark, but without my Katie there to protect . . . well . . . I just don't like the dark much."

"Yeah. It *is* kind of scary." The Rotten Willy nodded. "Especially when you have to sleep outside like I do. There's always weird noises and . . ."

"*CHUCK!*" Tom screeched.

I yanked my head round and glared up at him.

"What?" I snarled. "What is it? Can't you see I'm right in the middle of a conversation?"

His eyes were wide.

"You're on the bottom branch," he whispered out of the side of his mouth. "All he's got to do is give a little jump and he's got you. You're dog food!"

CHAPTER 9

Yes, sir! Best friends just don't come any better than Tom.

That made twice he had saved my life. Once, when I froze in the tree over Rocky's backyard. Again, when I was within reach of Rotten Willy.

Man—dogs sure are sneaky. You can't trust the things for a second. Most are loud and obnoxious and rude. They bark and snap and chase you, even when they know they can't catch you or even reach you. Others are real quiet. They try to sneak up on you. They lurk in the bushes, thinking you won't hear or smell them and will walk close enough so they can grab you.

Still others—like Rotten Willy—pretend to be nice. They try to get you to trust them, to drop your guard. Then . . . then, it's all over!

That's the way Tom explained it when I scampered up the tree to join him on his branch. For a time I wasn't sure whether this huge beast was a dog, like he said, or some strange animal called a Rotten Willy. Now, I was certain. Only a *dog* could be so sneaky.

And to think that I'd trusted him. . . .

Rotten Willy kept us in the tree for a long, long time. He kept asking stuff about the neighborhood, and if there were other cats and dogs besides us and Rocky. He said he smelled something good to eat and wanted to know what it was. Tom and I didn't speak to him. Hoping he'd go away when he realized we weren't falling for his tricks and coming down the tree, we just ignored him.

Only, he didn't go away. He curled up and took a nap.

When we heard the sound of Pat's car, we both yowled: "Mama, help! Mama, help!" Only Tom's Pat didn't hear us. She took a sack of groceries and went inside.

After a while, we heard the sound of another car. Rotten Willy perked his ears. With his little stub tail tucked tight against his fat bottom, he took off like a shot.

I started down the tree, but Tom stopped me.

"Could be another one of his tricks," he cautioned.

We stayed put. A little while later, we heard a woman's voice.

"Willy, did you do this? Bad dog! Bad dog!"

Quickly, Tom and I trotted across the limbs that arched over Rocky's yard. Like always, he leaped and barked his threats. I ignored him, like Tom had told me to. I kept my eyes on the branch and never so much as glanced down.

From Rotten Willy's tree, we watched as a woman-people shook her finger at the big, black monster. He lowered his head, and his stub tail pressed so tight against his bottom I could hardly see it. The woman-people got a shovel and filled the hole. All the time she worked, she kept scolding Rotten Willy and telling him: "Bad dog. Bad dog."

Tom laughed. I did, too—but only because Tom did. It wasn't much fun to get in trouble with your people. I felt sorry for Rotten Willy. Kind of sad for him, in a way. But since Tom thought it was funny . . .

With Rotten Willy hiding in his doghouse, it was finally safe for us to come down from the trees. We headed back to Tom's yard. Rocky barked and jumped and threatened. We didn't pay any attention. Once in Tom's yard, we each went to our own home in time for supper.

* * *

Every morning, when the Mama let me out, I headed straight for my best friend. Before we started our day's adventure, we always checked Rotten Willy. Tom could climb high up in his tree and tell me if he could see him. If he did, I would run around behind Rocky's fence to make sure there wasn't a new hole under Rotten Willy's pen. Once certain it was safe, we began our day.

On Mondays, Wednesdays, and Saturdays we went to the football field and made fun of the dogs. On Tuesdays and Thursdays we went to see Luigi, and ate his marvelous spaghetti and meatballs. Fridays were kind of open. Sometimes, Tom and I would pester Rocky. Sometimes, we would walk over and try to tease Rotten Willy. It wasn't much fun, cause he never got mad or barked and growled at us. Still other times, we just slept in the sun or lounged around all day. On Sunday, we stayed with our people. That was mostly because of Tom. The Daddy and Tom's Pat were all alone. Tom spent the weekends with them.

My Katie came home after being away for about three weeks. It was *wonderful* to have her home. When it was time for her to leave, the feel of sad swallowed her and me both.

It was four weeks before my Katie came to visit again. The leaves had turned colors and begun to fall from the trees. It always made me a little sad, because it meant that cold was coming. This time, my Katie was just as happy to be home, but she didn't give off as much sad-feel when she went back. The next time she visited, I was worried. She talked about a boy. Not the Jimmy boy, but a new boy. When she left, I could feel happy coming from her. I was afraid she might not want to come home. I was afraid she might forget about the Mama and the Daddy. She might even forget about me.

Monday, it was back to the same old thing. When the Mama let me out, I arched my back and stretched. Then I headed off to join Tom at the football field. Only Tom wasn't at the football field. I found him sitting in his front yard, staring at a big sign. I looked both ways and trotted across the street.

"What's it say?" I asked.

Tom shook his head, only he didn't look at me. He just kept staring at the sign.

"I don't know."

"Where did it come from?"

"Some people came, yesterday. They walked all over my house." He took his eyes from the sign and glanced at me. "I don't like strange people in my house. It makes me nervous." He looked back at the sign. "When they left, they put the sign here."

We stared at it for a long time. I wish I knew how to read so I could tell what it said. Finally, we gave up and went to make fun of the dogs.

It was afternoon when we got around to Rocky and Rotten Willy. Tom let me cross over Rocky's yard first. When he came over the branch, he acted like he was going to fall. Rocky went wild. It was hilarious.

We called Rotten Willy "Fatso" and "Lard Tail," only he just ignored us and curled up in his house. Tom crept clear to the bottom of the tree. I held my breath when he strutted over to Rotten Willy's house. He thumped on the side with his paw and raced back up the tree.

Rotten Willy didn't even look up.

"What's wrong with you," I meowed from the tree. "You weird or something?"

Rotten Willy opened an eye.

"Yeah." Tom jerked and flipped his tail from side to side. "Why don't you bark at us or chase us? You're a dog, aren't you? Aren't dogs supposed to chase cats and try to eat us up?"

Rotten Willy's paws were crossed. He flopped his head on them and stared at the ground.

"I guess I was raised different from most dogs."

I frowned at the top of his head.

"Who raised you?"

"Tuffy."

"Who's Tuffy?"

Suddenly, he made a grunting sound and turned around inside his doghouse. All I could see was his stub tail.

"Who's Tuffy?" I repeated.

In a very soft and faraway voice, he answered: "Tuffy was my friend."

That's all he said. We stayed in the tree for a while, but when he kept ignoring us, we left. On my way home, I glanced at the sign in Tom's front yard.

"Sure wish I could read." I shrugged and trotted to my house.

I guess it really didn't matter. Regardless of what the sign said, Tom and I were best friends. We would be best friends . . . forever.

Chapter 10

Me out! Me-out! Meeeout!"

The sound that came to my ears that bright winter morning was probably the most pitiful sound I had ever heard. I stopped. Listened. The cry made the hair tingle on my back.

"Meeeout! Meeeout!"

My eyes flashed wide. It was Tom's voice. Frantic and scared, it cut through the crisp air like a knife. I darted between the shrub and the house, raced around the corner, bounded over the rosebush and into my front yard. A huge car thing stood across the street. There was a big box on the back of it and bunches of wheels. It blocked my view of Tom's house.

"Meeeout! Meeeout!"

I raced across my yard. Almost to the street, a

sudden vision of Louie flashed through my mind's eye. My front legs locked. The pads on my paws skidded across the dry, brown grass— then caught. I stopped so suddenly that my back end lifted clear off the ground and my tail flipped up. The very tip of it thumped me on the nose.

Once stopped, I looked both ways. A car-thing whizzed past, not two feet from my nose. It stopped, then turned at the corner. It was a close call.

Certain that nothing else was coming, I charged across the road and under the car-thing with the box on the back. The instant I stepped from under it and onto the curb in front of Tom's house, I froze. Not even my tail flipped. Eyes wide, I could only stand and stare.

Tom's yard was a disaster. There were boxes and chairs and tables all over the place. Two big men with light brown shirts and light brown pants carried a box into the back of the car-thing. Two more men brought a couch from the house.

"What are you doing?" I hissed. "That's Tom's safe place. If you take his couch, he won't be able to hide when strangers come to his house. Where are you taking it? What are you doing?"

"Meeeout!"

My ears twitched. I looked around, trying to find where the sound came from.

"Tom? Is that you? Where are you?"

66

"Meeeout! Meeeout!"

The cry came from a pile of boxes near the garage. The men stepped from the back of the car-thing. I waited until they went into Tom's house, then raced to the stack of brown cardboard.

There was box piled upon box, with barely a path between them. I sniffed, listened, scampered here and there—still no sign of my friend.

"Tom, where are you? I can't find you."

"Here. I'm over here! Get meeeout!"

A gray box stood alone just inside Tom's garage. Made of shiny plastic instead of cardboard, it had holes in the sides and a wire gate on the front. Through the wire, I saw Tom's whiskers and his little black nose.

"Tom . . . what . . ." I panted, out of breath from my frantic search. "What's happened? What's wrong?"

"Chuck . . ." he panted back at me. I guess he was out of breath from all his meowing, and from being so scared. "Chuck. Get me out of here. Help me!"

I circled round and round his gray box. I even climbed on top of the thing. I stuck my paw in and tried to pull the wire gate open. There was no way in.

"I can't," I gasped. "I don't know how."

He sat down. I could see his wide, frightened

eyes staring through the wire gate. "Why? Why? Why?" he meowed. "They put me in here late last night. All weekend, they have been putting things in boxes. But I never dreamed they'd put me in a box. I'm not a thing! I'm their Tom. My Pat was the one who stuck me in here. She petted me and stroked my fur—then she told me she loved me. Then . . ."

Tom stopped. He made a sniffing sound, and used his paw to wipe the tear from his whisker. "Then . . . she put me in this box and put me in the garage."

I rubbed my side against his cage, trying to get close to him—to comfort him.

"I'm sorry, Tom," I soothed in my best purr. "I wish there was something . . . I'm so sorry."

It was all I could think of to say. There was nothing I could do to help him. Nothing, but stay with him until the men in the brown shirts and pants had loaded all the other boxes and all Tom's furniture. By the time they closed the huge doors on the back of the big car-thing, it was almost dark. Tom's Pat came. She shooed me away with her foot. She picked up Tom's cage and carried it to her car-thing. We didn't even have time to tell each other good-bye before she slammed the door in my face.

I stood close, hoping she would open the door again. Hoping she would roll the window down so I could tell my friend how much he meant to me. I stood close until the car-thing snorted at me.

When it roared and began to back up, I circled around in front of it and stood in the middle of Tom's yard. In the twilight of evening, I watched as it and the big car-thing with the box on the back disappeared around the corner.

Legs churning, claws gobbling up the ground, I raced to the end of the block. I stood and watched as the car-things moved farther and farther away. I watched as they grew smaller and smaller— until there was nothing left but a faint glow from the red taillights. Then—finally—the red glow faded into the darkness. I was all alone.

CHAPTER 11

Lonely just isn't any fun!

Lonely was a people-thing word. I had heard my Katie say "lonely" one time when she and Chuck stopped dating and before Jimmy showed up. I heard the Mama and the Daddy say it a bunch when my Katie left for the college place. I just didn't know what it was. Not until Tom left.

Louie got smushed by a car. My Katie went away. Tom got carried off in a gray box with bars on the door. I was the only one left. I knew what "lonely" was.

For a whole week, I didn't do much. When the Mama put me out back in the mornings, I ran around the house to see if Tom had come home. His house was empty. The sign was the only thing in his yard. I spent most of my time under the rosebush in front of our house. I watched. I jumped to my feet each time I heard a car-thing come down the road, then slumped back under the rosebush when it wasn't Tom.

Lonely felt empty and sad. I didn't feel like eating. The Mama worried about me. She petted me more than usual and stroked my fur. It didn't help.

The next week was pretty much the same. I ate better, but that was only because hungry hurt almost as much as lonely. After two weeks, I finally realized that Tom might never come back. I couldn't spend the rest of my life under the rosebush. Maybe I could find another friend.

The football field was no fun. There was nothing there but people and dogs. Teasing dogs wasn't fun without Louie and Tom. I went to Luigi's. He fed me and petted me. He asked about Louie again, and about Tom. But even after I told him what had happened, he kept looking around like he might see them. Wish people could understand.

One crisp morning when the wind wasn't blowing, I could hear crows calling from the pecan trees at Farmer McVee's. Tom and I had never been to Farmer McVee's. Louie had gone there once. He told us that there were huge monsters with teeth growing out of the tops of their heads. When he saw them, he ran away.

Maybe the monsters with teeth growing from the tops of their heads were gone. Maybe there was another cat who lived at Farmer McVee's house. Maybe I could find a new friend.

There was an empty field behind our house. I heard the Daddy say that someday there would be houses there, just like the ones near the football field and on our side of the block. When I started across the field, each step was slow and careful. I kept my ears perked. I kept my eyes moving and darting to catch the slightest movement—the first sign of danger.

The empty field really was empty.

After a while, my pace quickened. The grass was tall and hard to see through. There were strange smells. Suddenly, in the distance, I saw something. It was an animal. From here, it sort of looked like a cat. Cautiously, I eased closer.

The animal had pointed ears—like a cat. He had whiskers—like a cat. He was mostly black with a white stripe that ran down his back and tail—I had seen cats that were mostly black with white. Only, his tail didn't look like a cat's tail. It was full and bushy, and he held it straight up in the air instead of out behind. Still . . . maybe he was just a strange-looking cat. Maybe he would be nice, and maybe he would want to have a new friend as much as I did.

I flattened out on my belly. My tail jerked from side to side, but only a tiny bit. Not enough for the animal to see. Like creeping up on a mouse, I eased closer and closer and . . .

All at once, the smell hit!

My nose crinkled up. My tongue rubbed against the roof of my mouth over and over again, like it had a mind of its own and was trying to push the nasty taste away.

Whatever this black animal with the white stripe was—he was no cat!

Still crouched low, I made a wide circle around him. Once sure I was far enough away, I stood up and trotted on.

After a while I came to a fence. It was made of large squares of wire that were held up by big, brown poles. On the other side of the fence the grass was shorter and almost green—not brown and dead like the grass on this side of the fence. Another smell came to my nose. It wasn't a good smell, but not as bad as the one that came from the black and white animal. I sat in the tall grass and watched.

With the short grass in front of me, it was easy to see for a long ways. I waited and watched. Finally, I eased through one of the wire squares and started across the field.

"Moo!"

I jumped. The sudden voice beside me scared the tar out of me. I tried to leap back to the tall grass, only I landed crosswise on the square wire. I hit so hard that I bounced against it and landed even farther out in the open than where I had started.

Frantic, I scrambled to my feet and looked around.

"Moo!"

The huge beast was only a step or two away. The thing stood almost as tall as a house. It had an enormous, square face—even bigger than the Rotten Willy's. And sure enough—just like Louie had said—two gigantic teeth stuck out from the top of its head. It took a step toward me. I couldn't move. Humongous nostrils gaped open. They were big enough to sniff me in and swallow me whole.

"Don't eat me! Don't hurt me! What . . . what are you?" I stammered.

"Moo!" was all it said.

"I'm . . . I'm sorry. I don't understand."

"Moo!"

"What's 'moo'?"

The thing leaned closer. The two teeth on top of its head pointed down at me.

In the blink of an eye I spun, darted between the square wire on the fence, and raced for home.

I hid under the rosebush until well after noon. It took that long for my heart to quit pounding and my fur to flatten down. Whatever the thing was, I didn't want any part of it. It was so colossal, it was terrifying. But an animal who only knew how to say "Moo" and who had teeth growing from the top of its head—no way!

One thing for sure, I'd never cross the empty field again.

The next day I went to Luigi's for lunch. As always, he petted me and asked again about Tom and Louie. When I had licked the last drop of meat sauce from the spaghetti plate, I sat and washed my face. Only this time, instead of walking back home, I went around to the side of his restaurant.

There was a big, wide street in front of Luigi's. Car-things zoomed and whizzed past. One extra large car-thing, with a box on the back, whooshed so close that the wind from it ruffled my fur. Across the wide street was the shopping mall. But on either side and behind that were houses. Row after row of houses. Some had yards with fences. Others had no fence at all. It was hard to tell which ones were which because the car-things zipped by so thick that they kept blocking my view.

Still, there were bound to be pets there. Some of the people just *had* to have cats. With that many houses there were probably a world of cats to play with over there.

I waited. Watched both directions. Waited more.

For a moment, there were no car-things in front of me. The road was a wide, empty field of flat gray.

I stepped from the curb.

CHAPTER 12

Panting and gasping for air, I crouched beneath a bush at the side of Luigi's Restaurant. The car-thing had come out of nowhere. Like a streak of lightning—it appeared, then was gone.

Louie had saved me.

I had just stepped from the curb when a vision of him flashed through my mind's eye. I saw him all smushed at the side of the road. I saw him just as Tom and I had found him. The memory hurt my insides. It made me feel sad and lonely. But mostly, it made me step back.

The instant I stepped to the curb—that's when the car-thing came tearing past.

If there were cats at the houses on the far side of the busy road, I would never know. They couldn't be my friends. I would never *ever* go near the big street again—no matter how badly I wanted a friend.

I spent the next week beneath the rosebush at the front of our house. People came. None were Tom's people, though. They walked inside and looked around. Then they went away. More people-things came, but it was always the same. I heard crows caw from Farmer McVee's pecan trees. I ignored them. I went to Luigi's, only I always came straight home. I purred and sat in the Mama's lap in the evenings. She petted me, but only for a little while. Then she would shove me aside and work on her knitting. Mostly, I sat under the rosebush and just felt sorry for myself.

Then the most marvelous thing happened!

One morning, a car-thing pulled into Tom's driveway. A man-people and a woman-people got out. A moment later, a big car-thing with a box on the back stopped next to the curb. It had lots and lots of wheels. Men in light brown shirts and light brown pants got out of the big car-thing. Eyes wide and excited, I stood up. The men opened the back of the box and went inside. They began carrying boxes toward Tom's house. The man and woman opened the back of their car-thing. Even from where I stood under my rosebush, I could hear them grunting and struggling with something. With one final groan, the man lifted and turned.

That's when I saw them!

Shiny, slick boxes. The man and woman each had one. Not rough, brown boxes like the men carried. These boxes were smooth and gray. They had bars on the front. They were just like Tom's box. Almost exactly the same, only bigger.

I trotted to the middle of my yard. They carried the gray boxes to the garage. The place where Tom's Pat put him when he was in the gray box. I stretched my neck one way, then the other, trying to see who was inside. I knew it wasn't Tom. He would never leave his Pat or the Daddy. But maybe a new cat. Maybe two—maybe two new friends. The people were in the way. The men in the brown shirts put a couch between me and the garage.

I ran to the curb.

For a second, I could almost see. The boxes were in the middle of the garage instead of at the edge. Still, in the dim light I could almost make out fur and legs and . . .

The man-people closed the garage door.

As soon as they went to the house, I looked both ways, then sprinted across the street. I sniffed, but with all the oil and gas smell near the garage, I couldn't smell cat. I perked my pointed ears. No sounds came from inside.

I meowed. Again and again, I called to see if a cat would answer. With all the commotion—the men talking and clunking boxes around, feet pounding on the ground, the shrill scraping of table legs and chairs on the concrete—I guess the cats in the boxes couldn't hear me.

I was so excited I could hardly stand it.

My legs gobbled up the ground as I raced to climb the gate at the back of the house. The little door behind the garage was closed. I called and meowed again.

Still nothing.

For a good thirty minutes, I raced back and forth between the big door at the front and the little door at the back. The men kept carrying boxes and furniture inside or placing it on the lawn. But I knew that sooner or later they would finish. When they did, the man or the woman would open the door to the garage. They would let the cats out. I could hardly wait to meet them.

It seemed like I waited forever. I lay on a low branch of the pecan tree. That's where they would come. A tree would be the first place they would go when their people finally let them out. I washed my face. I combed my whiskers. I had to look my best when I met my new friends.

It was late afternoon when I heard the sound at the back door. I jumped to my feet. The lock on the door clicked. I sucked my tummy in. The handle on the door turned. I held my shoulders back, proud and handsome. The door opened. I smiled.

Like a streak, something burst from the half-open door. Two animals raced across the yard to the base of the tree—just like I knew they would.

When they stopped, my mouth flopped open. My shoulders drooped. My heart sank so low, it seemed to slither clear down to my claws and ooze out into the pecan tree.

"Hey, look what we got here." The fuzzy pink one smiled up at me.

"Yeah," the fuzzy white one said. "You talk about a neat housewarming gift. We got our very own kitty-cat." He licked his lips. "He looks kind of familiar, don't he?"

The pink—I mean, apricot one frowned. "Isn't this one of the guys who sat on the fence at the football field and made fun of our haircuts?"

The white one nodded. "Yeah. Told us that we looked like we were wearing a dress. Called us tutu-butt, didn't he?"

The two poodles began to circle the tree. They both looked up at me and licked their lips. "Come on down and play," they laughed. "Yeah. Here, Kitty, Kitty, Kitty."

CHAPER 13

The poodles circled the tree. They laughed and taunted, trying to get me to come down. Rocky leaped and barked his threats when I crossed above his yard. The Rotten Willy smiled up from where he lay in front of his doghouse. There was a little gap in the double gate at the far side of his yard. It was too far! I could never outrun the huge beast. My only chance was that the poodles would go inside at supper time.

They didn't.

I watched from Tom's tree when the woman-people brought their food. I called to her—begged for help. She didn't listen. Even when she put their food bowls on the ground, they wouldn't leave. First the apricot one went to eat while the white one stood watch beneath the tree. As soon as he finished he returned, and the white poodle ate while he stood guard.

I cried and meowed when I heard my Mama's car drive into our yard. She never heard me.

The night was crisp and cold. The sky was clear and there was no wind. I curled as tight as I could into the crook of the pecan tree. I shivered and wished I was home.

The next morning I crossed over Rocky's yard and sat in Rotten Willy's tree. I studied the crack in the gate. I crouched. Wiggled my back end. Then, I stopped and slumped on the branch. It was just too far.

That afternoon, the poodles ate outside again. Rocky ate outside, too. He sat on the far side of his food bowl and never took his eyes off me. Then I heard the door open at Rotten Willy's house.

"Help me!" I screamed, as desperate and frantic as I could. "Please help me!"

The woman-people put Rotten Willy's bowl down next to his doghouse. She patted him on the head and looked straight up at me.

She saw me! How wonderful!

"Help! Help!" I called. "The dogs have me trapped in the trees. Get me down. I'm thirsty and hungry and I want to go home. Help!"

The woman-people smiled. "Looks like you've got a new friend, Willy," she said. "I didn't know the neighbors had a cat." She rubbed Rotten Willy behind his ears and stood up. "You play nice with the little kitty, you hear me?"

My eyes flashed wide open when she turned.

"No! Don't leave! Don't go back inside. Help me. Help me!"

Then . . . she was gone.

Rotten Willy took a bite of his food. He opened his huge jaws to take another bite, then he stopped and looked up.

"You can have some of my food," he offered. "It's good. It's nice and warm, too."

My rough, dry tongue made my lips tingle as it traced a slow circle around my mouth. Then my eyes squinted tight. Just how stupid did this dog think I was?

The second night was worse than the first. It was colder, and the wind began to blow. From Tom's tree I watched the big, puffy, gray clouds. Us cats hate rain and snow. It makes us wet, and wet fur is no fun. Still, I wished it would rain. I even hoped the snow would fall. If it did, at least I could get a drink. I was dying for a drink.

Early the next morning, my Mama came hunting for me. I could hear her calling my name as she moved all around our house, then through the front yards on this side of the block. Hard as

I tried, I couldn't answer. My mouth was so dry, I couldn't even meow. Despite the wind that made the limbs rock and shake, I made my way over Rocky's yard. The poodles smiled up at me. They licked their lips and called: "Here, Kitty, Kitty."

Rocky leaped and barked when I crossed over his yard. My legs were weak and shaky. I almost missed the jump.

Gasping and trembling all over, I stood on the branch for a long, long time before I could go on. I was so thirsty and hungry that my paws didn't feel right. They wobbled and shook with each step. I moved carefully. Easy—one paw in front of the other.

Just as I made it to the place where the limb joined the trunk of Rotten Willy's tree, I stopped. My pointed ears perked up. My whiskers and tail, both drooping low with my misery, sprang straight.

That's when I saw it.

Far out on the tree—almost to the alley—a limb hung low. It swayed and bobbed up and down with the push of the wind. As it went down, it almost touched the wooden fence between Rocky's yard and Rotten Willy's. I frowned, studying it for a long, long time. The top of the fence was narrow. It would be like walking a tightrope.

Maybe late in the evening, the wind would stop.

It was almost dark when the wind finally settled. It never stopped. The limb I watched never quit bobbing up and down. Still it was calmer than during the day. Night would provide good cover. If I did slip, maybe Rocky and Rotten Willy wouldn't see.

It was my last chance. My only hope.

I scampered for it.

Okay—I didn't scamper. My insides told me to scamper, but I was so weak it took me forever to stagger to the limb. It took even longer to ease my way out onto the swaying branch.

My weight pushed it down—only not quite close enough for it to touch the fence. I reached out a paw. I felt the wood, then the wind lifted me. When the limb dipped low again, I reached farther.

This time it held. I put my front paw on the top of the fence. My legs shook beneath me. I put my other paw on it. As my weight came off the branch, it began to rise.

I couldn't turn back!

I had to go!

The instant my hind feet left the limb, it sprang back up and bobbed in the wind.

Trembling, I managed to balance on top of the fence.

An inch at a time—one wobbly, shaky paw after the other—I moved atop the narrow wood rail. It wasn't much farther. Just a few more steps and . . .

WHAM!

The wood boards shook beneath my paws. Frantic, frightened eyes looked down. Rocky leaped against the fence.

WHAM!

My hind legs slipped from under me. Claws sprang out. Desperately, I grabbed hold of the wood. For only an instant, I dangled there—right over Rotten Willy's yard. If I could just pull myself back up. If I could just . . .

WHAM!

I fell.

The world spun for a moment. Paws, claws, tail—all spinning, all trying to grab something, *anything.* Then I hit the ground. The world spun again. Only this time the spinning was inside my head.

Run! Move! a voice screamed inside me. *Get up! Get away!*

It was no use. The fall had knocked the wind out of me. I was so weak and tired and thirsty, I could barely lift my head. And when I did lift my head—that's when I saw him.

He was enormous. Brown on his chin and two tiny brown spots above his eyes, the rest of the huge beast was black as death. He came from his doghouse. His monstrous paws shook the ground. I could feel the vibrations beneath me as he rushed nearer.

Rotten Willy stood above me.

My eyes scrunched tight. My fur ruffled when he sniffed. I peeked from one eye. His jaws were wide. His enormous, white teeth were as long as spears. I felt the hot dampness of his breath.

Closer.

Closer.

The gaping cavern of his mouth was a bottomless pit. His jaws began to close.

I squeezed my eyes tight. *Please,* I prayed. *Please, please don't let it hurt.*

Then everything went black.

CHAPTER 14

My prayer was answered. Sort of . . .

I was cold and wet. Really cold. I had always hoped that there was a Cat Heaven. And if there was, it would be green and pretty. There would be fat, juicy mice all over the place—more than enough to go around for all the other cats. It would be wonderful and . . . warm.

My eyes fluttered. I still felt cold and wet. Nope. This wasn't Cat Heaven! But what? Where was I?

I was on my side, so I struggled to my feet. I coughed and sputtered. The sound of running water came to my ears. I looked around. So much water dripped from my left side, it looked like a waterfall. The water streamed down, splashing in a small pond. Made of white plastic, the pond wasn't very deep. It only came about two inches over my paws.

It was the Rotten Willy's water bowl.

My wet whiskers sprang up on one side. I had to get away. I had to make a break for it. My tongue touched the water.

I wanted to run, only my tongue wouldn't let me. It took over. It slipped out of my mouth and scooped up the water, then darted out again and again and again.

I almost had my fill and was ready to run when . . . well . . . there's nothing quite like the feel of a big dog breathing on the back of your neck. I glanced up.

Gentle as a butterfly's wing touching a flower, the Rotten Willy's jaws wrapped around me. He lifted me and plopped me down in another bowl.

Again, my head told my feet to run—to make a break for it while I had the chance. Only, the corner of my mouth touched something. My tongue darted out and scooped a tiny bit of the tasty stuff into my mouth.

"I knew you would have to come down from the tree sooner or later." Rotten Willy smiled and sat on his haunches. "I saved you some food."

My whiskers wiggled as the taste of meat filled my mouth. Cautiously—watching him out of one eye—I leaned to peek at the food.

"The Mama always mixes meat with the dry stuff. I would have saved you some dry food, too, but I got hungry." He ducked his head and gave a sheepish grin. "The meat is the best part, anyway. Go ahead. It's yours."

I was so cold, I knew I was going to shake myself clear apart if I didn't stop shivering. Still careful and watching his every move, I leaned over the bowl and began to eat. Water, dripping from my wet fur, fell and mixed with the food.

When the meat was almost gone, I peeked at the gate. Just one more bite and I'd make a run for it. Fast as I could, I'd . . .

The instant my eyes left the gate and glanced up, I saw his gigantic jaws close around me. Gently, he took me to his doghouse and plopped me on the floor.

Cats can see really well in the dark. Still, it took a moment for my keen eyes to adjust. That's because Rotten Willy lay in front of the doorway. He was so huge, he blocked it completely.

"What are you doing?" I gasped.

"You'll never make it." His voice was soft and gentle.

"Huh?"

Rotten Willy looked at me out of one eye. He raised his head and sighed.

"I said, you'll never make it. I could tell you were getting ready to run. You're too cold and wet. It's late at night, so your people are already asleep and they won't let you in. It's going to snow, and you'd freeze before morning."

I frowned at him and cocked my head to the side.

"So?"

"So . . ." Rotten Willy made a grunting sound when he plopped his head back on the floor. "You sleep here tonight. Go home in the morning. I won't hurt you. I promise."

How long I stood there shaking, I don't know. Finally, I got as far away as I could and curled up in the corner of his doghouse. I was so tired and weak, I couldn't even dry my fur with my tongue. My eyes were heavy, but I couldn't drop my guard. I had to stay awake. It felt like somebody put sand in my eyes. I blinked a couple of times. You've got to . . . stay . . . awake. . . .

"Would you be still?"

The voice snapped my eyes opened. I didn't even realize I'd been asleep, much less curled up right against the gigantic monster.

"I can't sleep with you shaking my doghouse."

"I can't help it." My teeth clicked together. "I'm cold."

Rotten Willy shoved himself up on one elbow so he could reach me. Then he began to lick, drying my fur with his huge tongue.

Dogs *really* have bad breath. I mean, it's horrible! But after a while, my shivering stopped. I was tired and weak and still scared, but my eyes felt so heavy I could hardly hold them open. I curled up against his tummy.

Again, I woke with a start. Blinking, I looked around to see where I was. The Rotten Willy was wrapped about me like a blanket. I was curled against his tummy—warm and cozy as could be.

I had no idea how long I had slept, but the ground was covered with a blanket of white. I could see it through the crack between his neck and paws. More snow fell. I could hear the soft, feathery sound as the flakes landed on the roof.

"Why are you being so nice to me?" I whispered, not sure if he was awake or not. An enormous brown eye peeked at me, but he didn't answer.

I leaned forward and stared at the eye. "Dogs chase cats. Dogs eat cats. That's the natural way of things. But you don't. Why?"

He snorted and plopped his head back on his paws. I leaned closer to the eye.

"Is it because of Tuffy?"

The eye glared at me. Then it closed tight. I crawled over his huge legs and stood, staring down at the closed eye.

"You told me that Tuffy was your friend. Did she make you be nice to cats?"

"I don't want to talk about it." He raised his head and turned it toward the doorway. I climbed up and put my paws on his cheek. I stood, staring down at his other closed eye.

"Why?"

The eye opened, but it didn't look at me. It stared off into the darkness of the doghouse.

"Because."

"Because why?"

"It makes me sad to talk about Tuffy. It hurts to even think about her." He closed his eye again.

I stood, watching him for a moment. I remembered the way Tom and I felt about Louie. How we missed him, and how we tried not to think about him.

"Did Tuffy get smushed?"

His massive head gave a tiny wobble.

"No. She just got old."

"I had a friend named Louie. He got smushed. I sure do miss him. I remember, one time when he fell out of the tree and landed in Rocky's yard. We thought he was a goner, but . . ."

It worked. I told him about Rocky and Louie, and I told him about how Louie was going to swat the Pomeranian on the nose—only he couldn't tell which end was which. And I told him that—sometimes—it helped to talk. And that talking made the hurt not be so bad.

He sighed and rolled back over so he could look at me.

"I was only a baby when the people-animals took me and my brothers and sisters away from our mama," he began. "They put us in a pet store. It was really cold and smelly and lonely. But my David found me and brought me home. I loved him and we played a lot, only at night I couldn't sleep with him. I had to sleep outside. That's where Tuffy lived. Tuffy was an old cat. I think she was a Si-mon-ese."

"Siamese," I corrected.

"Siamese?" he asked. "Mostly white with black ears and a black tail?"

"Yeah," I nodded. "That's a Siamese."

"Anyway," he shrugged his ears, "she was old and cranky, but I loved her a lot. Tuffy was kind of like a mother. She washed my face with her tongue. She scolded me if I had an accident on the floor. Tuffy played with me. One time, I got too rough and wouldn't mind her. She pounced on my head and bit me on the ear. It was nice to have someone warm to sleep with. This one time, after I got pretty big, I smarted off to her. Man, she jumped right on my back and . . ."

The rest of the night, I listened to him talk about Tuffy. I could feel the love from him. I could sense how much the old cat had meant to him as he thought of her.

Early the next morning, I squeezed through the crack in the big double gate and went home. The Mama was happy to see me. She fed me and told me over and over again how she was afraid something bad had happened to me. She even let me sleep inside when she left for work.

The next day, when she let me out, I went to see my friend. Rotten Willy and I talked about my Katie and his boy David. We talked about the college place. We took a catnap—I guess you'd have to call it a dog-and-catnap—inside his house. And that afternoon we played chase in the snow.

I heard my Mama call, but I stayed with Willy. He missed his David as much as I missed my Katie. It was nice to have someone to talk to.

In the middle of the night I woke up and glanced beside me. The beast was enormous! He was huge! With little tufts of brown around his mouth and over his eyes, the rest of him was black as death itself. On top of all that, his breath smelled bad and he was . . . *a dog!*

Dogs are loud and rude and noisy. They'd just as soon fight with each other as us cats. Dogs and cats just *can't* be friends!

My tail flipped—first one way, then the other.

Okay, so think of him as a Rotten Willy—not a dog. Nothing says you can't be friends with a Rotten Willy. The thought made me smile. Gently, I reached out a paw and touched his gigantic nose. A humongous eye peeked up at me.

"You ever eat spaghetti and meatballs?"

Willy raised his head and frowned.

"What's that?"

"You mean, you've never had spaghetti and meatballs."

"No."

"You're gonna love it. I got this people-friend named Luigi. He makes the best spaghetti and meatballs you ever sank your teeth into."

ABOUT THE AUTHOR

Among the many animals on the family farm in Oklahoma, BILL WALLACE and his wife, Carol, have a Persian cat named Gray. Gray seems to fear nothing and is usually "Mr. Cool" in any and all situations. Except when their daughter, Nikki, and her husband, Jon-Ed, come to visit with their two Rottweilers.

Gray instantly puffs to a huge fur ball and races for the nearest tree. Even when the dogs are locked in the pen, he stays jittery and nervous. Despite Nikki's assurance that the dogs just want to play, nothing can convince Gray.

Bill thought that maybe if Gray would just take the time to talk things out, like Chuck did—well . . . who knows.

Bill Wallace's novels have won nineteen state awards and made the master lists in twenty-four states.

Fulton Co. Public Library
320 W. 7th St.
Rochester, IN 46975